D0198877

A Cake for Gran

by Damian Harvey
and Srimalie Bassani

90710 000 435 108

It was Gran's birthday.

"I want to make a birthday cake for Gran," said Asha.

"I want to make this cake,"

said Asha.

"I'll help you," said Dad.

Dad looked at the cookery book.

"We need some eggs," he said.

But Asha dropped them.
"Never mind," said Dad
and he got more eggs.

"We need some milk,"
said Dad.

"Can I pour it?" said Asha.

"Yes," said Dad. "But be careful."

Asha poured the milk

into the bowl ...

... but it went on the floor.

"Never mind," said Dad.

"I will clean it up."

Dad put the flour and
the butter into the bowl.
"Now we need the chocolate,"
said Dad.

"Oh no," said Asha.

"The chocolate has all gone."

"Never mind," said Dad

and he put in bananas.

"Now we need to mix it," said Dad.

"Can I do it?" said Asha.

"Yes," said Dad. "But be careful."

Asha started to mix ...

but the cake mix went everywhere.

"Never mind," said Dad.

Dad put the cake into the oven
and Asha licked the spoon.

"Happy Birthday, Gran,"
said Asha.

"Here is a cake for you."

"Did you make it?" asked Gran.

"Yes," said Asha.

"And Dad helped."

Dad smiled.

Story trail

Start at the beginning of the story trail. Ask your child to retell the story in their own words, pointing to each picture in turn to recall the sequence of events.

Start

Independent Reading

This series is designed to provide an opportunity for your child to read on their own. These notes are written for you to help your child choose a book and to read it independently.

In school, your child's teacher will often be using reading books which have been banded to support the process of learning to read. Use the book band colour your child is reading in school to help you make a good choice. *A Cake for Gran* is a good choice for children reading at Blue Band in their classroom to read independently.

The aim of independent reading is to read this book with ease, so that your child enjoys the story and relates it to their own experiences.

About the book

Asha wants to make something special for Gran's birthday. She spots the perfect cake in Dad's cookbook, but it turns out to be much harder to make than it looks!

Before reading

Help your child to learn how to make good choices by asking: "Why did you choose this book? Why do you think you will enjoy it?" Look at the cover together and ask: "What do you think the story will be about?" Support your child to think of what they already know about the story context. Read the title aloud and ask: "What does Asha want to do? How do you think her plan goes?" Remind your child that they can try to sound out the letters to make a word if they get stuck.

Decide together whether your child will read the story independently or read it aloud to you. When books are short, as at Blue Band, your child may wish to do both!

During reading

If reading aloud, support your child if they hesitate or ask for help by telling the word. Remind your child of what they know and what they can do independently.

If reading to themselves, remind your child that they can come and ask for your help if stuck.

After reading

Support comprehension by asking your child to tell you about the story. Use the story trail to encourage your child to retell the story in the right sequence, in their own words.

Give your child a chance to respond to the story: "Did you have a favourite part? What things went wrong? How did Asha feel?"

Help your child think about the messages in the book that go beyond the story and ask: "Why didn't the cake look like the one in the cookbook? Why is everyone still happy at the end of the story? What could Asha do differently next time?"

Extending learning

Help your child understand the story structure by using the same sentence patterns and adding some new elements. "Let's make up a new story. 'It's Father's Day. Asha wants to make a card for Dad. First she paints a picture, but the paints spill over. Then she adds some glitter, but it gets stuck on her hands ...' What happens in your story?"

In the classroom, your child's teacher may be reinforcing punctuation and how it informs the way we group words in sentences. On a few of the pages, ask your child to find the speech marks that show us where someone is talking and then read it aloud, making it sound like talking. Find the question marks and ask your child to practise the expression they used for asking questions.

Franklin Watts
First published in Great Britain in 2019
by The Watts Publishing Group

Copyright © The Watts Publishing Group 2019

Series Editors: Jackie Hamley and Melanie Palmer
Series Advisors: Dr Sue Bodman and Glen Franklin
Series Designer: Peter Scoulding

A CIP catalogue record for this book is
available from the British Library.

ISBN 978 1 4451 6798 5 (hbk)
ISBN 978 1 4451 6800 5 (pbk)
ISBN 978 1 4451 6799 2 (library ebook)

Printed in China

Franklin Watts
An imprint of
Hachette Children's Group
Part of The Watts Publishing Group
Carmelite House
50 Victoria Embankment
London EC4Y 0DZ

An Hachette UK Company
www.hachette.co.uk

www.franklinwatts.co.uk